I spend a lot of time on my own

Of course I watch the television

John Burningham

ALDO

Red Fox

Other books by John Burningham

BORKA (Winner of the 1964 Kate Greenaway Award)
HUMBERT
TRUBLOFF
CANNONBALL SIMP
HARQUIN
ABC
SEASONS
MR GUMPY'S OUTING (Winner of the 1971 Kate Greenaway Award)
MR GUMPY'S MOTOR CAR
AROUND THE WORLD IN EIGHTY DAYS
COME AWAY FROM THE WATER, SHIRLEY
TIME TO GET OUT OF THE BATH, SHIRLEY
WOULD YOU RATHER…
AVOCADO BABY
GRANPA (Winner of the 1984 Kurt Maschler Emil Award)
WHERE'S JULIUS?
JOHN PATRICK NORMAN McHENNESSY
THE SHOPPING BASKET

A Red Fox Book

Published by Random House Children's Books,
20 Vauxhall Bridge Road, London SW1V 2SA.

First published by Jonathan Cape Ltd. 1991
Red Fox edition 1993.
© John Burningham 1991.

John Burningham has asserted his right to be identified as the
author and illustrator of this work.

Printed in Hong Kong

ISBN 0 09 918501 6

and I have lots of toys and books
and things.

Sometimes we go to the park

and occasionally we have a meal out

which is nice

But then I'm on my own again

I'm lucky though. I'm really very very lucky because I have a special friend.

His name is Aldo.

Aldo is my friend only, and he's a secret.
I know he will always come to me
when things get really bad.

Like when they were horrid to me
the other day.

I'm sure they went away
because Aldo came.

Aldo takes me to wonderful places.
I'm not scared of anything
when I'm with Aldo.

I couldn't ever tell anybody about Aldo.
They would never believe me
and they would only laugh.

Sometimes I wish Aldo would help,
but he's only my special friend.

Once I woke up in the night after
a bad dream and Aldo was not there
and I thought Aldo would never
come to see me ever again.

But Aldo had only gone to get a story
which he read to me until I went to sleep.

I wish Aldo could be with me all the time.

Of course there are some days
when I forget all about him,
but I know that if things get really bad

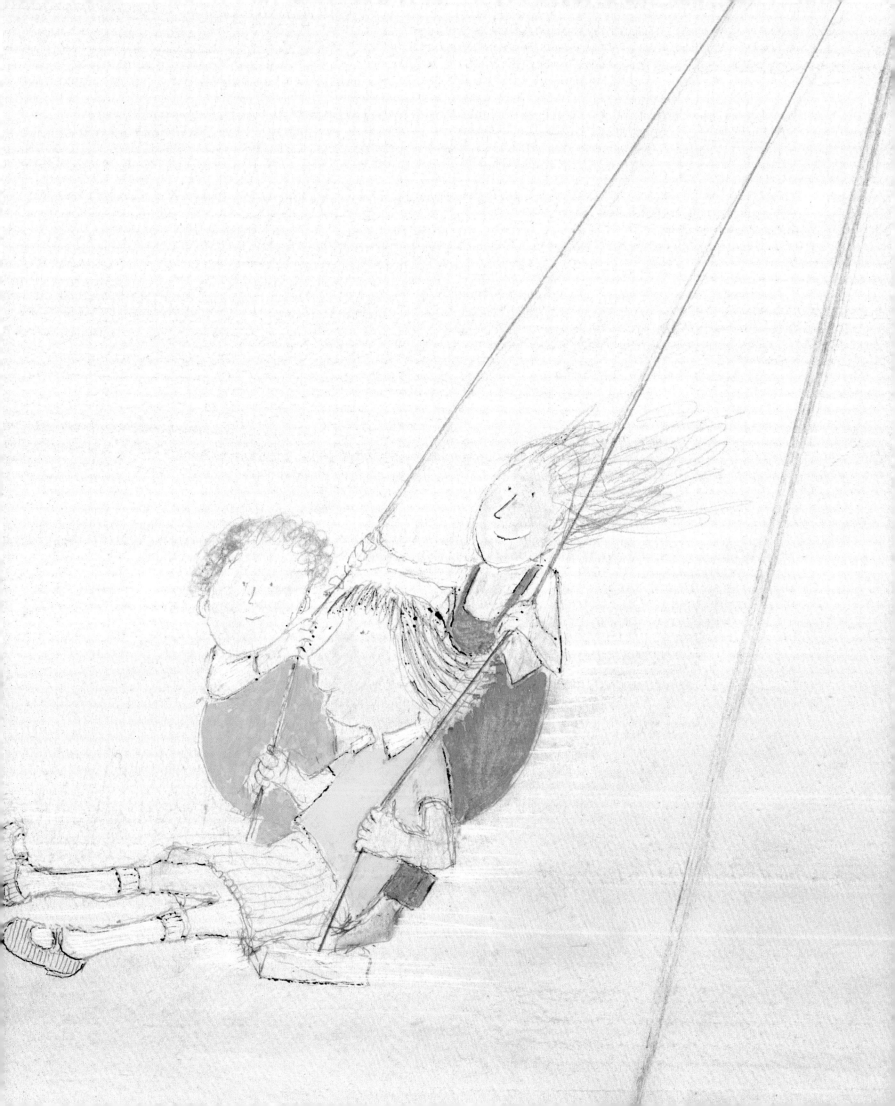

Aldo **Significant Author** will always be there.